The
Eroti

The
Erotic Way

Diana Riverside

SIMON &
SCHUSTER
EDITIONS

For Laurence C. Park (you know who you are)

SIMON & SCHUSTER EDITIONS
Rockefeller Center
1230 Avenue of the Americas
New York, NY 10020

SIMON & SCHUSTER EDITIONS and colophon
are trademarks of Simon & Schuster Inc.

The Erotic Way is produced by becker&mayer!, Kirkland, WA.
www.beckermayer.com

From *The Erotic Way* packaged set, which includes a feather, a silken cord, massage oil, a velvet mask, a scented candle, and this book.

Cover design by Michelle Keller
Cover photography by Lisa Spindler/Graphistock
Interior design by Heidi Baughman
Simon & Schuster Editor: Janice Easton
Edited by Lissa Wolfendale
Thanks to Gillian Sowell

Manufactured in China

10 9 8 7 6 5 4 3 2 1

Library of Congress Cataloging-in-Publication Data
Riverside, Diana.
    The erotic way : everything you need from stories to playthings for
an amorous, unforgettable evening / Diana Riverside.
       p.   cm.
    1. Erotica—Miscellanea. 2. Sexual fantasies. 3. Erotic stories.
    4. Sexual excitement—Miscellanea. I. Title.
HQ21.R57   1999   98-17303
306.7—dc21   CIP

ISBN 0-684-84883-X